Preface

When seeking to do anything good in life you will frequently hear the phrase, "Don't forget about me when you make it". Unfortunately, the real question should be, "Will you forget about me if I don't?" As life is filled with astounding transitions and adaptations, there are millions of things that are out of our control. There are, however, hundreds that are within our capacity and it's our job to seek and grasp things that are such. I hope this helps every reader drop their excuses and sense of entitlement, and assists in regaining control of their lives. This book includes over 100 years of practicality and wisdom from myself and numerous sought out professionals from all walks of life. I pray this book offers assistance in creating the most DYNAMIC version of you.

DEDICATION

We always ask ourselves, "So now what?" when life throws a curveball in our direction.

This book acts as a friendly reminder to myself while also being dedicated to student athletes, recent graduates, single parents, widows or anyone working on becoming the most DYNAMIC version of themselves despite struggling with the bad hand that life has dealt them. As humans, we must map out our plans and aspirations in pencil and give the man upstairs the eraser to edit when necessary.

CONTENTS

So Now What?

"Jerome "40" Howard tackles everything." "Forty with the touchdown." "Forty with the sack." "Turnover 40." "Mr. Third Down." These are some of the chants that echoed from the football stands for nearly a decade of my life. I was born on February 6th, 1993 as a native of Fort Lauderdale, FL, or what my peers referred to as "the crib". I earned the nickname of 40 back in high school while doing some additional agility drills after practice with one of my teammates, Cleve Williams. He was extremely competitive, outgoing, and always brought his energy into everything he did; practice, church, the weight room, class, etc. Although Cleve was wild at times, you knew exactly what you were going to get from him on a daily basis. Cleve started yelling, "There we go Big 4-0, there we go Big 40," and decided to continue with the name Big 40 for the next few days in school. As weeks went by, teachers and administration started calling me 40, as well. Even the faculty members who made the announcements on the loudspeaker in the mornings and at our sporting events hopped on board and were calling me 40. The nickname grew on me and I decided to keep the tradition going once I got to college and kept the jersey number 40. When my friends would come visit me at Prairie View A&M University (PVAMU), my teammates would hear them call me 40. My best friend, Terrence Mitchell (who went to Plantation High with me), was also on the team at PVAMU and would call me 40 constantly. Just like high school, my nickname made its way from my friends, peers and coaches all the way up to my professors. One professor I had was so accustomed to calling me 40 that he had to call the Head Coach of the football team to ask for my real name when entering my midterm grade.

The media has a funny way of showing you only what they want you to see. Take my hometown, Fort Lauderdale, for example; a great city for tourists, beautiful beaches & the place people go after they retire.

What people may be unaware of are some of Fort Lauderdale's most grueling cities such as Sunland, Tater Town, Parkway, Dillard, Driftwood, Lauderdale Manors, Melrose, Larkdale, Lincoln Park, Westwood, Deepside, Shallow Side and Royal Palm—just to name a few. We also can't disregard the neighboring cities-Miami and West Palm Beach—which also have similar misconceptions. The best way to paint a picture of my upbringing is to listen to "Love Yourz," by J. Cole. He says, "I grew up in the city and though sometimes we had less, compared to some of my homies down the block man we were blessed." Although I moved often in my younger years (usually due to financial reasons, such as landlords increasing rent, resulting in not being able to afford the unit anymore or the building no longer accepting the voucher we received from government assistance), we like most, had our rough moments, but I would have to say we were always blessed. There were definitely others who made our situations or problems seem minute. We had neighbors with nearly a dozen people sharing a one-bedroom unit, other neighbors who slept in their cars, and even some neighbors who struggled to pay the basic fare for local transit—which at the time was less than 50 cents. We did, however, have our issues, especially if a paycheck came even one day later than expected. I can recall situations where we would have to stay with relatives for a few days because of a delayed paycheck. Other times, we'd visit local pawn shops to temporarily pawn electronics or jewelry to get the money, and if things got better, we would have the option to go back and repurchase those items usually for the cost they gave it to you (plus a small fee on top). Usually after 3-4 weeks, if you didn't have the funds to repurchase your pawned items, you'd have to forfeit those items and the pawn shop could legally mark up the item and place it for sale in the store on their behalf.

My family and I did receive government assistance for my entire childhood (which at the time seemed like a nightmare or a never-ending run on a hamster wheel). However, in hindsight, there were many vital life lessons learned along the way. This upbringing supplied us with a daily dose of humility because, even though we had our good days, we were well aware of how life can instantly change, so we were forced to learn rather quickly about that happy medium of never too high never too low.

My mom was an optimist; she would always say, "You don't need money to be rich as long as you are rich in spirit". She'd also say, "Being rich in spirit is true wealth." As you can imagine, superficial things such as clothes, premiere shoe brands, and various other materialistic fashions took the backseat to more monumental things: family, loyalty, and faith. These three pillars were things my mom instilled in my siblings and I from a young age. Along with my siblings (Jamall and Janae), my mom would tell us that we were her everything and that life wouldn't always be this tough. Some of my most memorable childhood moments were holidays. We would just spend hours on end eating, dancing to the latest rap music, playing board games, or running around doing countless sprints barefoot in the midst of the summer sun (because we believed that my footwear was the reason, I hadn't won the previous two-three races against my other friends & relatives).

When you're younger, you're only focused on being a kid. As you grow older, though, your mindset starts to change and your focus switches to things like your financial status, career growth, stability, and living conditions. When you don't have significant guidance and aren't constantly exposed to role models or mentors, something else fills that void, usually leading to you creating a false ideal of what success is. Outside influences start to shape your interpretation of success and you start to believe that money and materialistic items are the only things that can have a positive impact on your life and make you "successful". Now you're stuck asking yourself, "How do I get money to change my situation?" For some, the answer to that question is unfortunately dependent upon the neighborhood you grew up in, and you're left with only three options: sports, illegal activities, or rapping. These are just examples of role models that my peers and I had access to. You would see your favorite athlete on TV and the glory that came with their fame—financial gains, helping their local communities—and hoped you could have that one day, too. Or you would hear similar stories from those doing illegal activities; what they did for the youth, like buying everyone something from the ice cream truck on a sunny day after playing sports outdoors, and hoped one day you'd be able to give back to your community just like them. These were also the same guys who would make sure to remind you to "stay in school" and "respect your elders". The last option, rapping, was a flashier lifestyle: riding around with rims on their cars, wearing big jewelry, and their car speakers so loud you could hear them coming from a few blocks away. Those were the three types of people my peers and I were exposed to, and the only ones who seemed to have escaped the vicious cycle of poverty.

For me, I found the answer at the age of six. I was introduced to football and began playing for the Lauderhill Lions, a team in the South Florida Youth Football League (SFYFL). At that time, the SFYFL was the top youth sports league. You had coaches who acted as father figures, team moms who helped assist in game day operations, and, most importantly, your first introduction to team culture and brotherhood. While I was playing football, my younger sister, Janae, would cheer, and my older brother, Jamall, who wasn't into sports as much, would be the team's water boy or our [Janae and I] security guard to make sure nobody messed with us.

Lauderhill Lions Optimist league Jerome Howard #00 (3rd row, fifth athlete),

I'm sure we can all agree that life has a funny way of pressing the fast-forward button, and you go from being a six-year-old kid to a teenager in the blink of an eye. Now you're picking out the clothes you're going to wear to school, experiencing changes in your voice, and you think you have this thing called life all figured out. You don't.

From 2007-2011, I attended Plantation High School (Plantation, FL) as a three-sport athlete. I was a four-year letterman with football, and I did track and field my junior year and wrestling my sophomore year. During my tenure at Plantation High, I went through years of growing pains, not just physically—growing from 5'6" to 6 ft. tall and going through puberty—but mentally, emotionally and psychologically, too. I was hanging around bad company, making poor decisions, had numerous in and out of school suspensions, as a result of either fighting or disregarding authority, and just doing things the way I wanted. In hindsight, many of my issues were pride related, alongside frustration, because I felt I needed attention and guidance, which just wasn't there at the time. I shuffled between living with my mom and my grandma who were hardly ever home. My mom and grandma wouldn't arrive home until nearly 6pm which was almost four hours after I was dismissed from school. They were usually so fatigued from work that their main concern was making sure we ate dinner, getting everyone prepared for school/work the next day, and getting some sleep before the cycle would repeat itself again. There weren't many talks at the dinner table about school, friends, or anything of the sort. They would ask if I had completed my homework (in which my answer was always yes), but there wasn't much proof or additional set of eyes on their end to verify that I had done it correctly or even done it at all. Often times, they would ask about report cards but we only received those every few months, so there was a huge grey area in between. Around the time they would see the report card, the damage would already be done.

I knew who I was raised to be, but high school can be a huge culture shock. I transitioned from this small pool of people of maybe a few hundred in middle school, to being surrounded by thousands of students daily in high school. Not to mention, in high school you start dating girls, earn scholarships, attend school dances and proms, have seven different classes and instructors, and are open to extracurricular activities after dismissal. While all of this is happening, you're trying to develop self confidence in a body that's rapidly changing. I mean, life really comes at you fast. I genuinely wanted to stay true to my parent's wisdom and disciplines, but their methods always seemed to be outdated in relation to my situation at the time. It was a daily struggle of trying to stay grounded on their upbringing and principles instilled in me or succumb to the pressure my peers put on me by constantly telling me who I should be.

I knew after my freshman year of high school that football was the one thing I loved and wanted to put all of my energy and focus into. After playing for nearly 10 years, it was still fun for me and it never felt like work. But there was still one problem.

When you start playing football at a young age it's all about having fun, developing a basic knowledge of the sport and finding early signs of athleticism. In little league, you're simply preparing the cocoon for the butterfly which will emerge later in life whether it be high school or collegiate sports. During high school, you actually learn more about specific positions, techniques, playbooks and sport IQ; many minute details are introduced, as well. Very early on in high school I had a second heart-to-heart with myself, coming to a realization that I had a massive problem: I wasn't that good. I wasn't the biggest, strongest, or fastest. Being 175lbs. I'd be running a mid- 5.3-5.4 forty-yard dash and that's probably with some assistance from the wind behind me. This is not only slow, but extremely slow. This would be accompanied by bench pressing roughly less than 100lbs for my one rep max. I started off as what I would call a "head scratcher". A head scratcher is one of those guys coaches look at and, while scratching their heads, wondering if this guy would fit on their roster or if he's even worth the investment. More times than not, the coach will just shout out the first position that comes to mind. Usually something like, "Hmm, yea, just join that group," pointing to a dozen other guys who he still wanted to keep in the same group but didn't figure out how to utilize them—or if they'd even be invited back the following practice. After minutes of pacing back and forth, squinting and twisting their hands through various planes of motions, trying to get a feel of my physical structure, my Junior Varsity coaches thought it was best for me to play offensive guard. My freshman year of high school, I would play offensive guard wearing jersey #73. I didn't know much about college and was just happy to be on the team, so anywhere the coach put me, I would give it my all to help the team succeed. Junior varsity games were on Wednesday's and I would attend the varsity games on Friday's and be amazed, thinking to myself, "One day that will be me". Seeing older Plantation High alumni, such as Josh Robinson and Brandon McGee, accept collegiate offers on signing day inspired me to strive for that same success. I never had anyone in my family finish college so that topic was a pipe dream to many of my friends with whom I shared my goals. I don't think they intentionally meant harm, but people fear what they don't understand. My friends were from similar upbringings so going to college, yet alone having such superior talents that someone would be willing to pay for your school in exchange for your athletic talents, was a fantasy because no one we surrounded ourselves with (friends and family) ever did. In fact, simply graduating high school was celebrated in my family as if one had received his/her doctorate degree. In order to have any hopes of that dream, I first needed to become a starter on the team, get rid of this number 73, and address the physical issues mentioned above. This inspired me to participate in wrestling, to help with my hip strength, playing low, driving my feet through contact, and playing with my hands to defeat the opposition (which would help in my transition from offensive guard my freshmen year to linebacker in the following years). I would later run track to help increase my speed, flexibility, core strength and body composition. I was fortunate to have a solid spring campaign. A need for more linebackers on the roster arose, so I was promoted to the varsity team as a sophomore. This was unusual because players would typically have to wait until they're juniors to be on varsity. I soon embraced my weaknesses and decided to work relentlessly on my craft. I would have frequent meetings with coaches asking for additional drills or suggestions on ways I can improve and applied them all. I even skipped out on lunch with my friends just to watch films with the coaches to improve my football IQ. This also taught me the process of how to watch films properly. I learned how to identify my weakness and how to put myself in the most advantageous position to capitalize on my strengths which were my instincts and IQ. I embraced the mindset of knowing, athletically, that an opponent may be more naturally gifted than me, so letting him get into open space without defenders on my team to assist me would not form a positive result on my end. The solution to that was to beat them to the point and use my instincts to meet the ball carrier within a few steps before he even had a chance to outrun me or juke me (which would be their strengths). Three years later, as a senior, I was named team captain and recognized as one of the top 50 players in Broward County, with scholarship offers from University of Marshall,

Central Michigan University, Western Kentucky University, Bowling Green State University, Alabama A&M University and Prairie View A&M University. While having these offers was a major accomplishment, they would mean nothing until the letter of intent is signed in February for national signing day. Gaining those scholarships were great, but I had a much larger speed bump to get over due to missing school a lot during my freshman year and falling into the rat race. The rat race is the term we used at Plantation High to refer to students who screwed up during their first or second year, and no matter how much they improved in their junior and senior years, the damage from their freshmen and sophomore years always placed limitations on how well their overall grade point averages would improve. This made things much more complicated on the back end. If you were able to get A's or B's during your senior year, it wouldn't really be reflected in your grade point average because of those bad decisions you made academically in the early years of high school. I needed to take night school and make up a few courses to make sure my core grade point average and my test scores matched the criteria needed to qualify for a scholarship. I worked diligently, sacrificing many nights of video games and fun with my friends, to hone in on this "once in a lifetime" opportunity. Come February of 2011, despite being committed to Western Kentucky University for nearly six months, I shocked the world and signed my national letter of intent to PVAMU in Texas alongside my high school teammate and best friend, Terrence Mitchell. My eyes were on the finish line at this point, with signing day behind me and four months left before relocating to Texas to continue my athletic career. However, what's life without surprises? I graduated in June and was merely two weeks away from departing from Florida to Texas to begin my collegiate career. Literally two weeks before my departure, I received a random call from the assistant head coach of Prairie View informing me that my arrival will have to be postponed as of now—and possibly canceled—due to me being audited/ flagged by the National Collegiate Athletic Association (NCAA). The NCAA was concerned about my "drastic" grade point average increase and how I acquired such good grades; they were curious if any foul play was happening behind the scenes to help me. The assistant head coach told me that he and the staff over at Prairie View would do their best, but in situations as such it's a matter of hoping for the best while preparing for the worst. So basically, in a matter of seconds, I went from one of the top signees for the Panthers to now being on the verge of forfeiting my scholarship and not even considered being on the team's roster for the upcoming season. To give you a visual, in the movie *The Blind Side*, the main character is sitting at an extremely long desk getting hammered with questions during an interview, later being asked to state in writing the courses he took, his selection process, and answer whatever other questions they threw at him. That was me.

I submitted the documents that the NCAA had requested and two months later (which seemed like 5 years) received another call from the assistant head coach who had some better news for me this time around: the NCAA granted me permission to go to campus, but there was a stipulation which they referred to as a 21-day probationary acceptance period. This would mean I would be allowed to arrive on campus and participate in practice, meetings, and all activities as a qualified student; however, if my case wasn't resolved by the 20th day, on the 21st day I'd be forced to forfeit my scholarship and return home at my own expense (as it would be a violation by the NCAA for the school to assist me in paying for my

travel back home if found guilty).
Through the grace of God, I made it to
day 18/21 and received the great news
that I was cleared and 100% good to go
at this point. They had seen that all of
my night school credits were legitimate.
Now If I would have remained focused
and made better decisions earlier in high
school, I wouldn't have had to be in that
situation where I had to take night
school or additional courses in the first
place. Once granted full clearance I
know I had something to prove. I used
all that adversity as motivation and a
lesson for future scenarios and attacked
everything with a mindset of "I'm here
to stay and I'm not going back home". I
had a great freshman season. I was
nominated a starter after my third
practice and brought what the coaches
called the "Florida swagger and nose for
the ball," which they said the Panthers
defense was missing the past few
seasons. November 12th, 2015 while
running down on a kickoff to tackle the
opposing ball carrier for the Alcorn
Braves, I tore my ACL, MCL and
Meniscus, later finding out that I would
need microfracture surgery. Clearly this
catastrophic injury put an end to my
season. Some of the coaches/medical
staff had questions and doubts about my
career. Through the grace of God and
working tirelessly, I found myself

working harder than ever to not only prove to the coaching staff that recovering from my injury was possible but to myself, as well. I would walk around campus to remind myself that I hurt my knee and my knee didn't hurt me, using that as a mental note that everything I wanted to obtain was still right there in front of me, and as long as I kept my mind in charge of my body and not the opposite, all of my goals were attainable.

I came back the following season, earned my starting position back and earned the respect of my teammates for my dedication and work ethic while I was injured, never allowing the injury to put me in the slumps as it had done to so many student athletes in previous years. I played the following season free of injury and led the entire team in tackles as a sophomore and earned the respect of many opposing coaches who would always share kind remarks with me after the game. Coaches would say, "Hey, man, I like the way you play" or "Hey #40, you got a bright future ahead of you." This would become my first year earning all-conference honors. During my junior year, I went out and played each and every game with a chip on my shoulder. Compared to my earlier years, things really slowed down a lot in my junior year and I was able to play and react even faster. I earned All-conference selection once again, all-American selections, and led the entire conference in tackles for loss. I would conclude my career for the Panthers as a 4-year starter, 3x all-conference, 2x All American, conference defensive player of the year my senior year, and current record holder for career tackles and career tackles for loss. Despite such accolades, good things don't last forever and my career concluded in college. I didn't receive an invitation to any NFL training camp and, in fact, only one team showed up to my senior pro day. A few days before the draft, the Tampa Bay Buccaneers scout called me verifying my contact info and said the team would possibly draft me if I was still around near the 7th round. That never happened and I never heard back from the scout after that call. I proceeded to do workouts for the CFL (Canadian Football League) after pro day and was told I would be signed by the Toronto Argonauts after one of their local workouts in Houston, TX. However, this was a mistake on their end because, despite needing a linebacker, the player drafted needed to be from Canada to stay within league regulations (and the league had a limit on the amount of American players permitted to each team). I did receive offers from arena leagues and teams in German, but felt none of those opportunities were right for me. Another factor was the compensation of $150 per game (which included the bonus if I was a part of the winning team). This just didn't sound too appealing to me. Even though the goal of becoming a professional athlete didn't transpire as I once wished during my tenure in college, something even better happened instead. I earned lifelong friends who I still speak to numerous times per week and, most importantly, I broke the cycle and became the first person in my family to graduate. I earned my Bachelor's of Science in Human Performance in the Spring of 2015. Everyone always asked if I'd forget about them when I made it, but it never dawned on me to ask them if they would forget about me if I didn't. Consequently, the common question I received for the next few years of my life—one that I even ask myself countless times daily—is "SO NOW WHAT?" …

I was in an awkward place in life. I felt misunderstood, betrayed, embarrassed, amongst a myriad of other feelings and emotions depending on which day of the week you asked me. So instead of wallowing in my sorrow, I started taking thousands of notes since graduation and I've spoken with hundreds of various professionals. Over time realizing, that I wasn't the only person feeling the myriad of emotions as mentioned earlier. This book will show you numerous concepts and principles that are applicable to sports and life that you should use NOW in your current state, along with a note to self for when life throws you a curveball and forces you to answer that recurring question, SO NOW WHAT?

NOTES

Chapter 1: Networking

Now that life has thrown us it's jab and we are aimlessly scratching our heads in disarray and frustration, the easy thing for all of us to do is to play victim to our circumstances and point the finger. Let's go ahead and throw away the paper listed with all of your misfortunes & excuses. Better yet, revisit the previous group messages you sent to your friends, wishing for pity and despair and delete them. At this point, there's no point in looking back because we aren't going that way.

Now that the ice is broken, let me share a fun fact with you: 80% of people don't care about your problems and the other 20% are happy you have them. We go around venting and looking for an open ear when most of the time the person on the receiving end is saying to themselves "better you than me". As cliché as this next statement sounds, one of the few things we can actually control is our attitude and outlook. Once we change our attitude, we are now able to view things at face value and realize in retrospect that the situation is probably not as bad as it seems; we just let our emotions get the best of us. Our revised outlook now allows us to identify opportunities for growth and improvement that may have been blinded due to our attitude. There's an old saying, "*Your netWORK determines your netWORTH.*" One thing I had to learn is that you can't do it alone and you would be naive to think anything less. I learned that behind every successful businessman, employee, manager, husband/wife, or elite athlete, is a list of screw ups followed by a mentor who has helped guide them. For those who perceive themselves as self-made, I respectfully ask you to think a little harder, and realize that at some point there was someone who helped you as well. Maybe your father wasn't the role model you would've liked or maybe your potential came off as threatening to others, so they didn't teach you things as you would have liked. But somewhere along your journey, you had *that* teacher, coach, neighbor, spouse, or even stranger who may have believed in you or even shared some encouraging words with you along the way. Fortunately, sometimes mentors can also be people who show you what NOT to do. You do not have to like the way your previous boss treated his staff or maybe you hated the way your father communicated, but these scenarios can inspire you to become that mentor you've always wanted once you get to a certain place in your career. If viewed correctly, all of those scenarios can be vital elements we can all add to our lives. One of my favorite sayings is, "If you see someone put their hand on the stove and burn it, and someone else follows along, continuing the same mistake, I think it would be wise moving forward to follow the road less traveled and not touch the stove." If viewed correctly, it can be an opportunity to learn from the mistakes of others and make a wise choice and save yourself the trouble, pain, financial losses, and, in some cases, your life.

Marquis Johnson is a certified strength & conditioning coach for the National Football League and works as the assistant coach for the San Francisco 49ers. Nearly a decade ago, Marquis was working numerous odd jobs, getting his hands dirty, simply doing anything legal that he could think of to make ends meet. One of his odd jobs was to drive the Pedi-cab to pick up & drop off pedestrians to and from the games or events in Houston, TX. If you're unfamiliar with a Pedicab, it's one of those bikes with the seats in the back where pedestrians can sit as the driver pedals the bicycle and carries passengers to their desired location in exchange for a base fare (and a tip if the service meets the passenger's expectations). One day, Marquis was simply doing his job—

routine conversation, networking, and dropping off a pedestrian to one of the Houston Texans football games. The client and Marquis connected really well, had a few good laughs, noticed a few similarities in one another, and decided to exchange contact information before parting ways. Marquis and the gentlemen would keep in touch over the years and grow their relationship. Fast forward nearly a decade after, that same client whom Marquis drove around on the Pedi-cab was granted the position as one of the coaches for the San Francisco 49ers. Can you take a wild guess on who you think he decided to be his assistant coach? Yes, you guessed it, Marquis Johnson. Marquis had no idea things would work out as such, but he always valued networking, working hard, and most importantly, being a good person. Marquis' scenario is a perfect example of the saying "It's not who you know, but who knows you." The coach could have easily gone with someone more certified or with more credentials, community service hours, or what have you, but there are some things you can't put a price on like trust and character. The coach knew Marquis valued humility and didn't mind getting his hands dirty, working late nights when needed; they gained a ton of respect for each other over the years. You can know whoever you'd like but the true question is, who knows you? In truth, if people don't know you and can't vouch for you then sadly, you're just another fan. There's a difference between being a smooch or kiss up and creating healthy and genuine relationships. If you think back to any of your previous dating relationships, I'm sure you can attest that whatever you do to get a position or title you will have to do that and more to keep your position. So, if you're buying flowers, going on lunch dates, or calling your significant other daily to prove your worth, then you have to do that and then some to keep a prosperous relationship. The same applies if your relationship is gained via networking. If gaining it involved you butt-kissing or smooching to get a position, well, sadly, you will have a long career ahead of you that will include those similar traits. As Marquis often warns me, value creating healthy relationships with nothing in return and no hidden agendas/ This is the key to longevity. Marquis says when you travel to an airport, you're seated next to a stranger for a few hours anyway, so why not start a conversation and open your mind to new concepts. You never know who you might meet, what you might learn, and most importantly you never know who knows who.

There are some people who don't have people checking in on them, asking about their day, or the last movie they watched. A simple compliment which requires little to nothing from us. Often times, your immediate friends (despite how highly you may think of them) may not be the ones to land you the dream job that you desire, so through genuine networking and being a good person, a friend of a friend may know someone and that person would vouch for you, possibly landing you an interview which can lead to a job even if there are people ahead of you who are more qualified. Networking can also work negatively if you're not careful. There's something called six degrees of separation. This is the idea that all people are six (or fewer) social connections away from each other, which results in a chain of "a friend of a friend" that can be used to connect any two people in a maximum of six steps. Thus, if you have a bad report, and just one person knows about it, it could end up negatively affecting you in the long run. For example, as an athlete, if you're a good person—but are always tardy, a terrible teammate, and often get in trouble— sure, you may get offered a scholarship and then possibly receive inquiries from an NFL team and, if you're really good, get drafted. If that's the case, congratulations on a great honor! However, let's say you're someone who they thought could be a late signee or late draft pick, you're off the field records can force you to go as a free agent instead of a draft pick. You become someone who is a high risk for an organization. Therefore, they'll take the business approach and aim to minimize their losses if their perceived notion of you is proven correctly. If you're someone of the opposite spectrum with that same talent level you may possibly get drafted much earlier, increasing the team's investment in you, the amount of money you can make off the field in autograph signings, appearances, and so on. Not to mention, in the case of an injury, an early draft pick or someone who they have money invested into has a better chance of remaining on the team due to the investment, whereas a free agent with less invested into the organization may be more open to counting their losses and moving on. Another great benefit of networking is that it allows you to expand your mind and horizons to new concepts and ideas that you may not be exposed to during your daily routine.

When was the last time you spoke with someone from another state?

When was the last time you spoke with someone from another country?

When was the last time you spoke with someone whose first language wasn't the same as yours?

If you need additional networking pointers I would like to suggest a few, such as going to a bookstore or a local library, occasionally catching the bus/train to work as opposed to driving, or instead of looking for the next post to screenshot to your friends group message, how about we change our perspectives and use social media to seek knowledge and connect with others. Let's be honest, we are all on our phones all day anyway, shuffling through apps such as Facebook, Snapchat, Twitter, Instagram, Netflix and Hulu, should I continue?

If you have been listening to rap/hip hop music for some time now, you probably have heard Drake's song "No New Friends." I'm a huge fan of Drake's work ethic along with his consistency in dominating the hip hop industry. I see his viewpoints from two different spectrums. Being around professional athletes and so called "celebrities" daily, I understand where he is coming from. Celebrities and people of status are approached constantly by people with what they claim to be the next million-dollar idea and only need a small loan or donation to convert those ideas to that next level. Next, there are those who are straight forward with their intentions, but will feel as if your blessings and gifts are theirs as well. Then there is another group of people who come around and pretend to be friends or "family" with you to ease into their proposition once your guard is down and you feel them to be no threat. This is a slippery slope, because now you're asking "well how do I know who is really for me and who is just pretending." Well, I've asked that question to a dozen influencers, coaches, and entrepreneurs; although they used different words, the common denominators in their advice were to trust your gut, as it's always undefeated, and to use your ears and your knees. Praying and paying attention to actions, people will reveal their hand eventually, we just have to be wise and courageous enough to believe them once they show you. Consequently, if you're not careful you can fall into that trap and start applying that Drake concept of "no new friends" in your life which can pay poor dividends in the long run. I will repeat again something from our opening statement: *your netWORK determines your netWORTH*. This next statement will hurt a lot of hearts but its paramount. Some of our alleged day one friends (referring to the timeline and duration of knowing the person) have been envious and hating on you since day 2 (referring to a much earlier phase in time). Yep, these are those same friends whose houses you had sleepovers at, carpooled to events with, attended the same church, shared clothes, and/or played on the same youth organized sports teams. Some people are only your friends because you're beneficial to them—you have something they want. Once those things don't reconcile, their friendship or loyalty to you utterly breaks down.

Coach Bubba McDowell, former seven-year vet and University of Miami student-athlete, states many times how, when he was playing, everyone loved him. He'd receive hundreds of fan mail and tons of free items from people because of his celebrity status. He says, in hindsight, he hardly ever heard the word "NO!" But once the air is removed from the ball and those three letters— NFL aka National Football League Aka Not for long—are no longer attached to your name, people will show you how they really feel about you. One of coach Bubba McDowell's favorite bible verses is Corinthians 13:11 which states, *"When I was a child, I spoke as a child, I understood as a child, I thought as a child: but when I became a man, I put away childish things."*

There comes a time when certain things you may have done in high school no longer interest you post-graduation, but we all have those groups of friends who are resistant to growth and continue to do things that you stopped doing years ago. Now they will say certain things like, "man, you changed" or "you're not real anymore" or the bell cow of them all, "you think you're better than everybody". Go ahead and smile, because the fact that you picked up this book lets me know that you are seeking personal growth and want to gain additional insight in some form of your life, so I know you've heard at least one (or maybe all three) of those phrases being thrown at you. The root cause of it all is you wanting more than your current predicament, whereas the opposite is true for them. There are some cases where both parties can be growing but growing in opposing directions (this is also fine). Our current generation struggles with accountability and is persistent with having an excuse for everything; thus, leading to a false sense of entitlement. Their issue really isn't with you, it's with themselves. We have two people, who grew up in similar living conditions and were given the same opportunities: one person decided to stays focused and on path to creating a better life while the other stayed stagnant. That's not your fault, it's theirs. Yes, you're acting different. You're growing and manifesting great things in life while they're looking at you with a sense of jealousy, because now they can't run to their excuses or alibis and are forced to look themselves in the mirror and gain a sense of accountability. This is very uncomfortable and shameful to many people. The elevation requires separation and many who start with you won't finish with you. Some of those childhood friends or high school friends were good for you back then. As you progress and move forward, you require people who are more compatible for the revised version of you. We should all value growth, and anything or anyone who doesn't contribute to that may need to be left behind. Many chose to point the finger when the real problem is the person looking back at them in the mirror. They'll come up with all the excuses but never take the blame. "Nobody else in my family did it so how can I?" "But my dad wasn't present in my life" or "nobody woke me up for work and my consistent tardiness caused my manager to terminate me, it's their fault for not waking me up." Let me be clear about something: there are some phenomenal friends out there and I'm extremely blessed to have two or three of them. But people have also labeled me as someone who had changed or acted differently , thinking im better than others due to having the opportunity to play football on the collegiate level (in another state) or because I chose to workout with my teammates and surround myself with people who have equal values and aspirations as I do. These are the same people who have just as much or even more than I to have to lose by making poor decisions. There were former childhood friends and members of my immediate family who would constantly make poor choices, only to find themselves in and out of jail, detention centers, and all sorts of trouble. The things I wanted didn't align with things they wanted, so to many of them I switched up and changed, or turned "Hollywood" as they liked to call it (referring to Hollywood, CA: walk of fame, flashing lights, etc.).

As mentioned in previous chapters, there is nothing wrong with making a new mistake. If I see that you burned your hand on a stove top, I owe it to myself to learn from your mistake and wrong decision by not making that stupid decision. We all should value and hold our friends and family very close to our hearts, but often times, it's actually a stranger or someone you may have had limited interaction with that will support you more than your friends. I believe this is because your friends may secretly be competing with you and quietly hoping you don't blossom due to their own insecurities. They want you to do well but it can't be better than them. You may have dreams of owning a home one day, and that's completely fine with them, but theirs has to be in a better neighborhood/bigger/generally nicer.

Being personable and having good networking skills you'll be able to make more of an impact and reach indescribable levels. During my collegiate days, student-athletes received meal plans that enabled us to eat for free in the campus cafeteria. The cafeteria was open to all students for breakfast, lunch, and dinner and twice per day on the weekend. There was one long table centered in the middle of cafeteria and was nicknamed "the football table." It became an unwritten law that if you weren't a football player or highly vouched for by a large portion of the team, then you didn't sit at the table and you'd simply admire from afar. To make matters worse, we created a certain stigma that football players only hung out with football players or other student-athletes from other sports, but you didn't bring around "regular people" because they weren't a part of the tribe and couldn't be trusted. Who did we consider a regular person? Anyone who wasn't a student- athlete. So even if you joined a fraternity or sorority, you were still considered a regular person. We created the stigma that regular people being too high a risk to us because we felt we didn't have anything in common with them—they didn't play any sports, so they were probably just trying to get close to us because they had a hidden agenda. That agenda could be getting free tickets, utilizing your free books due to your scholarship, getting some additional clout or recognition, getting girls, free football apparel, or gathering the inside scoop to spread to others. As an 18-21-year-old kid, it sure made a lot of sense. We had to protect the brotherhood and keep our guards up at all times. In the real world, this is a terrible decision simply because we all hang around people who we feel have similar thoughts and viewpoints as we do. Therefore, if you limit your netWORK you limit your netWORTH. You can become closed-minded feeling the athlete's way is the only way to do it. This is completely false, as there are often numerous ways to complete a task and those "regular people" are actually an asset to you. Sometimes when you're in the heat of things and trying to juggle so many different tasks—study hall meetings, group projects or competitions—you tend to overlook a lot of things. Our actions were also a poor choice of sportsmanship and gratitude, as the regular people were the ones who helped us out the most. Whether it was their money helping us with athletic scholarships or them selling out the football games, they always supported us and raised money for the team. Not to mention, post-graduation, "regular people" had helped me more than student-athletes. You may establish a relationship with a classmate during a group project or you guys may study together and they can open your eyes and give you some insight on things. There isn't one person who knows everything, so having an open mind is vital to our long-term success.

NOTES

Chapter 2: The Transition

The word patience can give many of us the chills just thinking about it. "You mean to tell me; I have to wait longer?" Patience is a virtue is valued much less in our current generation when technology and social media will make you believe that you'll get the body you want in a few days if you use this supplement or take this magic pill. This could not be further from the truth. As the introduction states, this book is also a note to myself. I've began praying for such things as wisdom, discernment, and patience daily. More often than not, when the product or destination is reached, many are happy that it took as long because there were certain growing pains, a skill set or mindset that we needed to acquire before getting that desired task (not to mention the extra baggage in the forms of people who we may have outgrown who are working as antagonists to our aspirations). What I've found is that if we look at the root cause of things, lack of patience really can work synergistically with insecurity or ego. We often feel we need to reach stardom tomorrow to show off our dream house or to showcase this facade of living a certain way, or even to compete with a neighbor or loved one. I have yet to find someone who enjoys eating lukewarm turkey on thanksgiving. In fact, we want out turkey cooked for extensive hours with the best gravy and accessories that can be bought. To confirm that food is cooked to perfection, we will measure the meat's temperature, and even try a sample ourselves. The same concept can be applied to our lives. If we don't count the cost and continue to chase our aspirations, we can expedite things. This causes us to reach things prematurely resulting in the same example of the lukewarm turkey. That lukewarm turkey leads to disasters such as stomach pain, nausea, vomiting, food poisoning—all of which are unpleasant.

There are certain tests and things that we need to develop thoroughly to create the most dynamic version of ourselves. One thing we can do is create a vision of long terms goals. Those goals should be followed by short term goals. If you view the long-term goal at face value, it can seem overwhelming and unachievable, or it may seem like it will take centuries to complete that goal, which will add more fuel to the fire of our lack of patience. Instead, if we focus little by little with smaller, minute goals, it'll make time pass by so much faster. ` An analogy that my dad enjoys (and reminds me of all the time) is driving on Interstate-95, which is one of the premiere highways in South Florida. Interstate-95 can take you from Miami, FL to Canada (and other neighboring cities). My dad would go on to elaborate that most accidents will come from the lanes furthest to the left, which are classified as the faster lanes. The lanes to the right are [usually] the lanes with new drivers from driver's education courses, elderly people, and, generally, the more patient and conservative drivers. With the implementation of cell phones, everything is caught on camera and some even feel that if "Instagram/Snapchat didn't see it then it didn't count." We are all one video or Snapchat post away from being "viral," as in being famous from a picture or video that is posted online and shared hundreds of thousands of times, sometimes millions. This again is a symptom of insecurities as I mentioned earlier. We want to "work hard" for 30 seconds, turn around and have all the treasures and glory as the person who has been sacrificing and working hard for 30 years.

All professionals interviewed agreed that the success is in the journey, and despite their current level of success, they wake up every day embracing the journey and to create their story despite doing their respective crafts 10-30 years. Hearing the stories of many of my mentors and the sacrifices they made to reach their current skill level in their professions, I found myself picking my tongue up from the floor just imagining the grueling things they overcome. Patience is a virtue and patience does builds character. I believe we can all remember a time where we really wanted something, where our emotions almost got the best of us, but we practiced having a little bit of patience and it ended up helping us in the long run. Timing is imperative!

Read the following questions below. Before you answer, close your eyes and really think about your response before writing it down. Could you have imagined meeting your significant other when you were a freshman in college and just happy to be out on your own? If you're not in college yet, just imagine meeting your spouse at age 18?

While there are exceptions, I think most of us would agree that we needed a lot of self-care and life experiences at 18 to help us become a better person which would lead to becoming a better spouse. Let's be honest, it's not that he/she was a bad person. It's simply because you may have overlooked them due to timing and/or a phase you were going through. Most people would probably call you crazy if you met someone at the bar and were engaged to them three days later.

Your friends/family would say you haven't invested enough time or you're moving too fast. Am I right?

As a fitness professional, I have some extensive conversations with many people concerning exercises to target an array of body parts. I can speak to you about sleep, recovery, hydration, pre/post workout nutrition, supplementation, you name it. If I don't know you, give me 48 hours and I will have a more informative answer for you thanks to some good mentors. Just like a lot of us spend tons of hours in the gym, working on our training and working on personal aesthetics, patience requires some exercise as well. Our exterior surface can be as healthy as can be, but our patience may be out of shape and desperately crying out for help. Patience is a great gem to have in your tool box because it allows you to empathize. Sympathizing for someone is usually more superficial (feeling sad for them or being concerned). Empathy is more about having been in his/her shoes before and having concerns, because you know what they're going through. Patience gives you the ability to empathize for others because there aren't many new problems; simply new victims. So, you can now become someone of value or even a living testimony (for lack of a better term) due to your ability to connect and empathize from your own personal experience.

To be clear, lack of patience isn't an excuse not to have goals. In fact, I believe that your goals should be so big that they'll scare you. We only have one shot at this thing called life, and I feel that we owe it to ourselves and all of those who believe in us to dream amongst the stars. Your dreams should be so wild that you feel uncomfortable telling them to small-minded people or those who may not see things the way you see them. If you haven't done so I challenge you to write out a few long-term goals (for a few years down the road) and then some short-term goals.

NOTES

As any great teacher will tell you, everyone learns differently. You have auditory learners who hear things, relate it to a sound and then the light bulb goes off and they'll complete the task at hand. Visual learners learn from seeing things and painting a picture in their head, whereas kinesthetic learners learn from experience, moving around, allowing those situations to help get things done. According to studies, the majority of us are visual learners. Maybe it's time you actually put your goals on a vision board or even a small sticky note on your office desk. There is no right/wrong way here. The visual paper or board should address both long term and short-term goals. This can be accompanied by a few actions & small goals along the way to help hold you accountable. The same principle applies in the fitness realm: a client comes in with improper form and struggles to do the exercise with their own body weight, but with consistency and a little patience, they can eventually add weight. For some clients, the additional load may only be a resistance band while others may be able to add 5-10lbs. These both can lead to larger gains long term, but if you don't attack the smaller goals, then you'll quit prematurely, not seeing what greatness is in store for you down the road.

Another facet of having patience is having faith. The term faith is defined in biblical terms as the things hoped for and not seen. We are told to walk by faith and not by sight, so despite what may seem monotonous to your eyes or current perception, adequate faith is supposed to kick in and give you that assurance that things will work out for your good. Even when things may seem disastrous to the naked eye, good old faith kicks in giving us yet another reason not to give up, allowing us to give it one more shot. Despite coming from a family who would treat the church as their second home - spending infinite hours at the church from teaching bible study, singing in the choir and/or cooking in the kitchen after services if needed, there comes a time in everyone's life when they have to break away from their parents beliefs in order to make their own. You have to go out, make experiences, develop your own faith and get more in tune with that spiritual or higher power in which you believe. You can stand, shout, and get temporarily inspired by others situations, but you must put forth the effort and work on developing that own faith of yours. Faith and Patience are siblings, meaning they both go hand in hand. It's very hard to have faith without having patience because if you aren't patient, you aren't in line with practicing faith. If we put too much emphasis on when we believe things should happen, we can get in our own way (as I so often do).

Before we get too far ahead of ourselves, I would like to be clear that by no means am I pushing Christianity or any religion on you; I respect all religions and all forms of spirituality. To my understanding, every religion promotes optimism and utilizing your unique gifts for the betterment of the people. I have gained insight from numerous professionals who have coached or mentored some of the world's biggest & strongest athletes. One common denominator for all of them is, despite the athlete's height, how fast they ran a mile, how many certifications they held, their record breaking 40 yard dash times, how many words they could type per minute, how many times they lift 225 lbs. at their local pro day, or how low their body fat percentages are, they are all limited within what they can do as humans. I'm sure you have been through some things that have made you say, "life's not fair". Some of those blows may come with little effects such as a pinch on the wrist, while others may have been gut-wrenching, like the big drop of a roller coaster leaving you gasping for air in disbelief. In fact, tell me have you ever felt like sometimes when aiming to do the right things, and attempting to be a good Samaritan, life seems to reward us with more negativity? Not only is this frustrating but it's also come off as manipulative, and can cause you to want to revert back to your former ways. Various research/studies have shown sleep is very important and plays a vital role in human performance. What we fail to realize due to the fact that we're usually not conscious is that intensity of darkness is not uniform throughout the night. This misconception is a result of the limitation of the naked eye, which assumes that darkness is darkness and there's no variation in intensity. Thomas Fuller quotes, "the darkest part of the night is right before the sun rises". This implies that there's usually some turbulence before the calm, some difficulty before the breakthrough, and some labor before the delivery; but the secret is consistency and perseverance. I'm not perfect; in fact, I take pride in calling myself a perfect imperfection, but I do know that if I keep pushing through that dark time, even when things get darker, it means I'm only a speck away from the sunrise and things working out in my favor. As the old saying goes, *"tough times don't last, tough people do."* We have to find that superior power on a spiritual or energetic level that will get us through, because on our own, we are insufficient.

Now I may sound contradicting initially, and these next few paragraphs may require some additional reading, but I feel that sometimes we can have too much faith. For my spiritual indulgers, don't put the book away yet, hear me out with an open mind on this one. I would like to say that we can put too much on God. Faith is amazing and can open doors for you beyond your wildest dreams, but as the Bible states, *"faith without works is dead."* We can pray for things but if we don't put any action behind our prayers then we are doing ourselves an injustice.

Bubba McDowell, former NFL athlete and current coach at PVAMU, speaks about how many student-athletes come into college with hopes of obtaining a degree while also making it to the pros. Unfortunately, many will wait until their final athletic season has concluded before realizing they should've flipped the switch and did all of the things they should have done earlier in their career. We spoke earlier about pro day, where the student-athletes who've completed their senior season of football, or have decided to declare earlier (leaving college to go to the pros), get a chance to go out and showcase their talents to pro scouts through various drills that measures quickness, speed, explosiveness and strength. This is usually a one-day event that takes place after the national NFL combine, which is televised nationally. There are 300 candidates who will get a combine invitation—many from premiere colleges who have most of their games televised throughout the year. For the smaller schools, or candidates at your premiere schools, not going to the NFL combine doesn't eliminate your dreams. Scouts will also visit your school and you may be asked to join a bigger school near you for your pro day. The bonus for combine is the exposure of being on TV, but your pro day gives you a chance to redeem yourself if you didn't perform as well as you thought you should have. Many training facilities offer pro day training, where they'll prepare you in a tri-planar fashion physically, mentally, and emotionally in everything ranging from interview prep and physical performance to mentally handling the chaos that comes along with the process of becoming a professional. If you perform well during your pro day or at the NFL combine, NFL teams can reach back out to you and/or your agent and ask for a private workout in which they'll fly you to their facility. While all of this is great, the training period is usually 6-8 weeks in duration and reduced if you're someone who is dealing with injuries or nominated to play in an all-star game. If you decide to take workouts for granted, do the bare minimum to get by, make poor nutritional choices, and ignore the extra film study and various sacrifices it takes to become professional, it usually catches up with you down the road–especially on the smaller level of Division1-AA schools such as PVAMU, where your performances aren't displayed or televised on the national level unless you make it to the playoffs. We spoke about faith earlier in the chapter, believing things are possible. There is a point of faith when you have to do your part as well.

You can't allow the term faith to be an excuse for laziness. Bubba likes to recite from the word saying, *"When God sees you doing your part, developing what He has given you, then He will do His part and open doors that no man can shut."* He says we are children of the Most High and He doesn't want us to fail or give us more than we can handle, so if you are showing you don't have the discipline to manage time and prioritize things accordingly, usually with little to no money or income as a student, why should he trust you with millions of dollars, extensive off-seasons, and unlimited distractions? This would seem insane and detrimental to the man upstairs to do so. As a parent or sibling, you wouldn't give your teenage child a sports car at the age of 13 because you know it's too much for him/her to handle and the risk doesn't outweigh the reward. The man upstairs works in a similar fashion. If you go to your doctor's office and fill out the paperwork—usually pertaining to symptoms, blood work, allergies, liability waivers, etc.—you may initially seem annoyed or frustrated at the ridiculous amount of work and questions being presented, almost asking yourself, "why am I even here? isn't this the doctor's job ?" This couldn't be farther from the truth. In fact, you're actually assisting the doctor and, more importantly, yourself because, when the ordained time presents itself and it's your turn to see him/her, now the doctor can do what he needs to do to assist you. The doctor will know which medications, he can or can't prescribe, (additional screening if needed) and other procedures/task to get you to optimal efficiency. So, in other words, we have to work while you're in the waiting room.

Sadly enough, the world doesn't operate on the snap of our fingers or at our demand. Therefore, we have no timeline on when or how things will come to fruition, but what we can do is work diligently, so when the time arrives, we are ready. Have you heard someone praise how lucky they are? Well, to be lucky, he/she had to have been prepared for this "lucky" opportunity that presented itself. As Coach McDowell says to all of his athletes, always remember the five P's: proper preparation prevents poor performance. If you don't prepare yourself for the opportunity, then shame on you when it presents itself, and don't blame anyone but yourself when you aren't ready for the opportunity. We have to do our part in having faith, while working and putting some action behind that faith. We can't use faith as an excuse to settle for mediocrity. When God sees you doing your part, developing what he has given you, He will do His part developing doors no man can shut.

Write down three goals that you have always wanted to achieve.

Next, take some time and ask yourself what can YOU do NOW to improve your current situation to bring those plans to fruition? I will help you out by giving you my first answer.
• PRAY

Finally, this one will involve you digging a little deeper, ask yourself if one or all of the goals you mentioned came to fruition exactly how you wanted. Whose life (not including yours) would you change and how?
(Answer these questions before reading the next questions)

- Review your answers, particularly the final question. Few things in life are definite. Sadly, one of them is death. We're all going to leave this planet one day so let's re-evaluate some of our goals if they are only for our personal empowerment. I think we should identify our gifts and allow those gifts to make an impact on someone else. I believe in you, now it's time that you do the same.

Chapter 3: Mindset

It's your fault! Yes, all of it. Perhaps Michael Jackson's song, "Man in The Mirror," can provide some clarity here. Michael states, "I'm fighting with the man in the mirror, I'm asking him to change his ways." You cannot continue to do the same thing and expect a different result. That, my friend, is INSANITY! Accountability has taken a backseat to entitlement and flat out laziness in our current generation of millennials, and I think it's time we do away with the endless excuses and take back control of all things within our capacity to reach our destiny. To be clear, no one owes you nor me anything in life. We were fortunate to open our eyes and breathe this morning, which means we were given another chance. That alone is suffice beyond words because there are many who had plans for today but those people didn't get the opportunity to open their eyes today. Since we were granted the gift of life today, it's best that we show gratitude by displaying good effort and work toward being better today than we were yesterday.

Bruce McGraw is a man of many hats; a father, leader, divisional manager, community activist, and someone I'm fortunate enough to call a mentor. Bruce has a blue-collar work ethic, integrity, and old-fashioned grit. He's also a native of Fort Lauderdale but traveled thousands of miles to Huntsville, Alabama to attend Alabama A&M, majoring in electrical engineering. While that was his degree and interest in college, Bruce like many of us who graduate from college and develop a new outlook on life, changed careers over the years. Although he didn't have all the answers at the time (and attest he still doesn't), Bruce knew he wasn't going to sit back in sorrow and play the blame game; instead, he stayed positive and made the most out of his current situation. Bruce originally started working for United Postal Service (now referred to as UPS) at the age of 26. Bruce started off part time with UPS being one of three jobs at the time. Electrical engineering is a tough profession and can be hard and extremely competitive post-graduation, especially if you don't have much practicality or someone who can vouch for you to get yourself into the workplace. Therefore, Bruce worked numerous jobs to make a living while trying to figure out his next move in electrical engineering. His first job was a surgical tech assistant at North Ridge Hospital, handing the surgery instruments during operations. His next would be at Trey Winds Park in Coconut Creek, FL collecting fees as the visitors would enter the park. His third job would be at UPS.

As a newlywed who accepted the job at the UPS just months after marrying the love of his life, Bruce was aiming to get things afloat for himself and his future family. His initial role was in the warehouse loading the tractor trailers. He thinks back to those early days at UPS and says those were some hard times that seemed to make time go by slowly, and "your eyes would play tricks on you sometimes because you're consistently doing the same thing over and over only to notice 13 minutes or so would have passed on the clock." Bruce wanted something more competitive, somewhere he'd be able to push himself and become less monotonous. He laughs, saying he remembers, after the first few days, the weekend coming and he had a talk with himself, "If they have me on the line on Monday morning when I come in, I'm going to quit and just continue working my other two jobs." While those were his thoughts based primarily on emotion at the time, he kept his thoughts to himself and reflected back to his collegiate football days saying, "well I can't go in there calling shots, I'm the freshman on the job and will have to get in where I fit in at the moment." So, he revamped his thinking and came in ready to do the dirty work to earn his stripes. Ironically, Monday morning came and there was a shortage in another department (which allowed him to move from unloading the tractor trailers to go work on the purple belt). The purple belt would change his job responsibilities to now loading the trucks. This transition may seem tedious to some but to Bruce, he embraced it and enjoyed being able to be more hands-on. The feeling of seeing trucks come and go, gave him a sense of achievement and hunger to repeat the process with the next one as opposed to the previous job that just seem repetitive. He'd made a conscious effort to avoid drama and negativity, keeping to himself, reporting to his location and completing his tasks with maximum effort. As the new guy in the new location, he was just ready to work and get things done. Bruce was completely unaware at the time that his new job was less than 10 feet away from the divisional manager's office. His work ethic and keen attention to detail caught the eye of the divisional manager, leading to his name coming up in team meetings when he wasn't around. This would later lead to a future conversation between the divisional manager and Bruce about his interest in becoming a part-time supervisor. The paperwork was submitted and roughly a week later Bruce got his promotion. Once again, he continued working hard, arriving early, and giving it his best everyday: this led to another raise.

Within two years, Bruce had received three promotions, one leading him to be a supervisor at another location (adding another 35-45 minutes to his commute to work or around an hour and fifteen minutes with traffic in the afternoons when he left). Often times, Bruce would stay an additional hour or so to allow traffic to slow down and to review work. After 33 days as a supervisor at the Deerfield location, he was promoted to full time supervisor. Bruce says he remembers speaking with the payroll department after receiving his first full time check because he couldn't believe the increase in pay and believed the job had made an error or were playing some sort of prank, testing his integrity. The funds turned out to be exactly as intended. Bruce decided to let go of one of his jobs and continued at UPS working full time while also working on the weekends at the park for another 5 years or so. In 1993, UPS decided to add Saturday shipping and Bruce would become manager and be responsible for three counties which averaged, roughly, 3-4 full time supervisors, 100 employees, and 10 part time counties. This would lead to another pay increase and would now include stocks/shares within the company which were an additional incentive along with his base salary and bonuses. The great part about this was that if the company did well, they'd give their employees additional stocks as holiday bonuses and Bruce's shares would now double (since he continued to grow within the company). As with many people, they see this as a dream come true and fall into the trap of satisfaction, feeling they've made it and they relax. Bruce never got caught up in his previous successes and kept his eyes on the required task or project. In 2006, he was promoted to divisional manager, which would equate to another annual raise, and would now be earning triple the shares of a full-time employee and double that of a manager (which he was previously). In modern times, the standard age of retirement is between 59-65 and most people don't think long term when they're younger. This leads to them not having enough savings to retire, shifting all of the stress to their loved ones to carry the slack. Bruce was ready to retire at age 55 but his wife still had four more years to go, so he decided to make a promise to her: he'd work two more years. Bruce retired from UPS in 2017 with 29 years of work with the company. Bruce also earned the National Best Divisional Manager award twice in his time with UPS. He credits his journey to the man upstairs, his wife's unconditional support and optimism, his mindset, never getting comfortable, and always wanting more. Many In his position would have been content very early in their career, usually leading to decreased work performance or some form of mediocrity over the years. Bruce grew up in some of those rougher areas of Fort Lauderdale and his mother only had a third-grade education. She couldn't assist him much with his homework after he advanced past the third grade but she did value hard work & gratitude. His mom once told him, "I may not be able to assist you much with your homework, but I just ask that you do your very best and I will be okay with that." In retrospect, he says that mindset from gratitude and never getting comfortable was applied to all aspects of his life. From work and friendship to his personal life, as he has been happily married to the love of his life, Norma McGraw, for what is now approaching 34 years and counting. Bruce is living proof of the fact that despite where you come from, having the right mindset and the right team of people around you, anything is possible.

The game is played above the shoulders

Our Mindset plays a huge role in perception and the way we view things. When things happen to you in life do you automatically assume the worst possible scenario?

If I poured you a beverage and stopped at the midway point, would you view the cup as being half full or half empty?

Do you view the cup as half empty and never half full?

If answered half empty in the first question, and you admit to being one who sees negativity as the first option, that mindset can be regarded as a pessimistic one. Don't panic. With some work and consistency, your mindset can change. We can't approach this situation as we do with our new year's fitness goal where we start strong and dwindle along the way. We must start right now, irrespective of our imperfection.

Now that the problem is addressed, we can now focus on the reason for it being a problem in the first place. My generation, "the millennials," as highly as I would like to think of us, the sad truth is we are soft and overly sensitive compared to previous generations. I know some of us are a little stubborn, but if this book is able to change one person's mindset and outlook on life, then our mission has been accomplished. Read and repeat these words out loud: "I (say your name), will no longer play victim to the things that life throws at me. Yes, there will be good days and there will be bad days, but as long as I continue to wake up, open my eyes, and breathe, that means there is still a purpose for my life; otherwise I would just be useless and my presence on this earth would have expired by now. But since I am here, this should be a reminder that there's something is still out there for me." Now reread that past sentence. As mentioned at the opening of the book, this is also a self-reminder, as mindset is a category of infinite maturation. There is no finish line to growth, only countless adjustments and transitions. You feel a little better, don't you? Do you feel like you want to give it one more try? Well, so do I. So, let's grow together.

Take a look at the image above. You will see the horse, an extremely strong animal, has the perspective that it's stuck to the chair. We can subconsciously create a perspective in our mind that can cause us to forget about strengths and ability to choose, yet magnifying our inabilities. It's time we take back control of our lives. If the horse would get out of its own head, he would realize that he could do whatever he wanted and bring the chair along with him until it falls off at some point. However, many of us prefer the easy way, which would be to stay where you are, do nothing, and make excuses for failure. You have to be careful about what you tell yourself and the things you're thinking about. You can use the spiritual realm, law of attraction, positivity, energy or whatever works for you, but it is imperative that you feed yourself positive thoughts. Whatever you put into the universe comes back to you. Your energy speaks for you before you introduce yourself, especially if you're a negative person. We've all met people who were always negative and complain about something constantly (yes, that person you're currently thinking about). Those are the people who you should strategically avoid or distance yourself from, because we know their energy isn't what we would like to be surrounded by. Refer back to the networking chapter: would you want to do business, vouch, or even spend extended time around a negative person? Absolutely not! Just like many diseases, it's contagious and will rub off on you, and people will notice, which can inhibit certain blessings that should come your way. If you stay around negative people, their energy can be detrimental to your success as well.

Let's take a look back at chapter 1 again, networking. "It's not what you know, but who you know." Yes, your degree is amazing—I'm not diminishing your degree—but let's assume you're applying for your dream job and they'll be accepting applications for the next few weeks. Why should they give you the career opportunity? What do you think you can or will present to the company that none of the other 400 applicants didn't? You can't be that naive to think that your degree or years of experience will be the golden ticket at the theme park, right? Now let's imagine you have a relationship with the hiring manager, someone in the Human Resources department, or you have someone that puts in a word for you and vouches for you. All of sudden, your resume and application gains a second look (in some cases, you can even get hired without an interview).If you're someone who is always showing up on time, getting the job done and going above and beyond when needed, and you reach out to the hiring manager letting them know that you have someone for that open position who is similar , if not better, than they are, I highly doubt the hiring manager will think twice about giving you a call/interview on the spot. This is why your network and knowing the right people is so crucial. 1. This is a win-win for them because they don't have to micromanage you while also trying to complete their own responsibilities.

Culture is huge in many organizations as many people log in about 160 hours a month in their job and this number usually doesn't include weekends, or staying late in the office, meeting company deadlines. With that being said, no one wants to be surrounded by energy killers or slackers who don't complete their part, causing an inconvenience to everyone and causing you to dread coming to work. So, if they get someone who has good qualities and shares common outlooks, they'll help create a better workforce, increase productivity, and family-like culture at their job.

The best investment?

If you ever take time to think and jot down your long-term goals, there's a great chance that someone has done that before and you can seek wisdom from them. With the large epidemic of online lectures, seminars, and podcasts being produced daily, we have tons of blueprints to follow to get guidance—and oftentimes inspiration—from their journey. The main problem is we've grown lazy, and it's very important that we step up and work instead of feeling that the world is supposed to take care of us because we didn't come from the richest family. Sure, maybe your parents didn't have a trust fund for you, maybe your parents never finished college, but your background doesn't determine your destination. There are millions of people whose parent didn't go to college, let alone finish high school, yet they persevered and made a name for themselves through diligent discipline and grit. Even if you entertain the "lucky" term that many like to label others. There is still groundwork and preparation that had to be completed so you will be ready when the opportunity arrived. Instead of investing in ourselves whether it be saving more money, investing in your jobs 401 plan or IRA, continuing education for work, reading more or even exercising, we do the complete opposite. We have these big ideas of what we want to do "one day" yet there's rarely any true application toward that goal. What we should be doing is picking up a book more often. What we are doing instead is nothing productive, in or out of work, like rushing home to watch reality TV (which provides us with absolutely no return on investment).

We have what are called assets and liabilities. Assets are things that bring in monetary gains and/or something of value. Liabilities are bills, services or something that keeps losing value and poses high risk. Most wealthy people will explain to you that your greatest asset is TIME! We all have 24 hours in a day so if you invest your time reading, studying for your next exam, saving money, contributing to your retirement fund or future business, then you are investing in yourself. But if you decide to rush home to spend all of your time on the latest blog sites, partying every weekend, at endless happy hours or playing endless hours of video games, you are investing into liabilities—all things that will hinder your personal growth. It also shows that you aren't using your time optimally. If assets were deposits into a bank account and liabilities were withdrawals, once we withdraw more than we have in the account we go broke, or worse, we overdraft. There needs to be a balance and everything should be done in moderation. We owe it to ourselves to enjoy life and the hobbies we've picked up—and will learn—along the way, but if you review your past few days and didn't do anything to invest in your future, then you will get exactly what you put into it. If you know anything about compound interest, then you know that even what many would view as minimal or small gains accumulating over time will create hulking measures. At first, they seem needless and pointless. For example, deciding to read for 10-15 minutes a day to build your reading endurance. You may feel minimal gains or like you're wasting time. Overtime, you will improve your reading skill, while also improving the duration of reading. You will begin to knock out books in a matter of weeks. Then the 10 minutes per day compounds into 20 minutes per day which leads into numerous books read annually. No different than building your home—it starts off as laying that foundation, brick by brick, exactly how you want it and overtime you add more bricks until one day you look up only to realize that you have created your new home.

One extremely overlooked investment is your health. You have heard it before and I will repeat it again, "health is wealth.". I have been blessed with the opportunity to train some amazing people from numerous professions—NFL athletes, NASCAR drivers, police officers, youth athletes, collegiate athletes, hockey players, CEOs, entrepreneurs—and the underlying factor is that all of them, including myself, are nothing without their health. Due to lighting fast metabolism in our youth and early 20s, we're able to get away with certain things. As time goes on, though, that same topic of compound interest still applies, yet this time in the opposite fashion. Don't believe me? Well, let's view diabetes. You have type 1 and type 2 diabetes. Type 1 is usually hereditary and you're born with it without being able to do much about it. Type 2, on the other hand, is usually within your control and accumulates through years (roughly 8-12 years) of poor nutritional choices, stress, and sedentary lifestyle. We spend countless hours at work trying to finish the next project or praying for that next promotion or reaching deadlines that we usually let go of our own health. But over the years our health declines—clothing sizes increase, energy decreases—and we rely on the angles and filters on our smartphones to enhance our appearance. If continued long enough, your type 2 diabetes can sometimes become type 1 diabetes. This becomes unfortunate because all the hard work you did and sacrifices you made to finally get to a certain position or status will now fade away because of your health declining. You won't be able to truly enjoy the fruits of your labor or, as in many situations, you've accumulated more liabilities at this point, such as daily pills & prescriptions, increased insurance premiums & co-pays. You only have one life, so it's in our best interest to take care of our body & health which will be the vehicle of life driving you forward, allowing you to do certain things.

I got my degree!

If you have received your degree, diploma, GED or anything related, do me a huge favor and pat yourself on the back! I would like to let you now that your hard work did NOT go unnoticed and you deserve all the blessings headed your way. Now, I want you to imagine yourself being your favorite athlete in the final two minutes of a game and the score is tied up. There we go, give me that game face! Yeah, keep that because you're going to need it. The piece of paper (degree, certification, etc.) you earned is simply your admission to get into the theme park. Let's be honest here, due to strategic marketing from the media or campus advisors, you can be misled to feel that your degree is equivalent to crossing the finish line and people will be knocking at your door begging you to work for them. If you have ever been to an amusement park, you know there's usually a large crowd of people searching for their next ride (their next opportunity). When you're there, you usually have to dedicate almost a full day to enjoy all the rides. But (yes, there's always a but) ... the park usually offers VIP wristbands or express passes which enables you to skip the line for an additional fee or upcharge. The express users walk up to a different line than those who have passes for general admission, show the ride official their wristband and they get first selection on seats, walking around free of worry of lines and stipulations. Why? Because they got their passes.

There's a current stigma out that as long as you have your degree the real world would transpire in similar fashion as the amusement park. You have your degree, so getting a job once you graduate will be effortless. You'll interview for two or three positions and someone will be blowing up your phone with opportunities. WHY? Because you've got your express pass. Ironically, this couldn't be further from the truth. Use that degree as your ticket to get into the amusement park and once you're in, I've got two words for you; FAIR GAME!! You're actually the underdog because there are always other park members who will arrive before you. This means it's time to tie your laces tight, put on your game face, and hustle; it's time to go after all the rides and opportunities you want. Your piece of paper got you in the door, now you must apply the concepts from all the chapters discussed earlier. You must have faith that the weather will work in your favor and that your favorite ride you drove so far to experience won't have any technical difficulties, especially not when you're on the ride (I've had this happen to me before, not a good feeling). You must also be patient because there may be a long line of roadblocks which may cause a temporary stall in the ride. Networking and being open to new friends may provide you a shortcut or even a few more rides which you had no idea existed in the park. It also increases your confidence to conquer your fears/doubts and to actually get on the ride and not become inferior to your fears and/or anxiety.

Perspective is so important, and I think if viewed differently, we would understand that once you cross the stage or complete that certification, it's not the finish line; on the contrary, it's actually the starting point and everything prior was the warm up. What happens to many of us (including myself post-graduation due to student athletic obligations) is we don't attain any practical experience or internships in our major or area of selection so we graduate and just try to find jobs. Most jobs will want a minimum of three to five years of experience. The first two to three times you will think "it's fine, don't panic, maybe it's just those particular companies." Next, you may start to think that it's probably because of the field you chose and there isn't a huge need/demand in the workplace. Now you have to make a decision: do you change your major (if you're still in school) or enroll back into school in hopes of obtaining another form of education in a more demanding field. This will usually equate to significant amounts of student loans. To me, the most mind blowing of it all are the conversations you have with your supporting cast and often even yourself saying such things like, "how does everyone want me to have years of experience but no one wants to give me experience?" If that one didn't hit home for you, here's another one: how about searching for jobs related to your degree or previous job experience and hearing that you're underqualified for some of them—in which you feel you're worthy of them—while being overqualified for others. Both options lead to the job going with another candidate or not bringing you in for an additional interview. This can be heartbreaking, devastating, and can even play a role in you feeling a sense of betrayal and distrust from advice you were given over the years about the value of your degree(s). I'm not belittling the importance of a degree, as education and knowledge are imperative, but have you heard of the following companies Microsoft, Facebook or Apple? There are a few commonalities among them;

the first is that they are owned by some of the wealthiest people in the country. The second being that neither Bill Gates, Mark Zuckerberg, nor Steve Jobs have ever boasted about their degrees because they don't have one. They decided that self-education was more important than a degree. Many with a degree lack the practical experience of actually doing the job and only have what the book tells them to do. What's worse, they will typically have to unlearn many of those protocols once in the real world. Many companies and brands have a set system or format in which they do things and if you can't break away from your textbook theory and adjust to their systems then you will probably not be there very long, if at all. Over time, they may want to hear you out about certain topics or experiences, but more times than not, you have to earn your stripes and put in the ground work before you can start to call the shots or make suggestions.

Self-education is imperative. This gives you a wider perspective on things, and allows you to invest in yourself. It's no different than school; the teacher assigns classwork and teaches you the basics and you're supposed to go home, complete your homework and bring it back to class or submit online before an assigned time. That homework is you investing in yourself. There aren't many places that have the time to teach you everything you need in a classroom, so you have to take that initiative to do and want more. The outliers who do—such as the ones who advance faster at their jobs—obtain and provide more value to themselves and the company.

EGO = edging God/good out
PRIDE= purpose ruined in desire of ego

If you ask anyone who is an advocate of religion/spirituality they would often recite that faith and worry cannot live in the same house. If you pray, you should have faith it's going to work out and not worry. You can't pray and worry, you have to choose one. Well, that same token must be put into application when you speak of humility and pride. A prideful person is a disaster waiting to happen. The acronym stated in the title breaks down pride as "purpose ruined in desire of ego" and ego can stand for edging God out. If you're someone who doesn't believe in God or there is a different name for the spiritual power you believe in, we can use the phrase "edging good out" and get the same message across. Pride and confidence are two things. Yes, you should have confidence and dignity about yourself and your craft. However, there is a very thin line between confidence and arrogance. Once you reach the point of closed-mindedness and having a sense of arrival which no longer accepts corrections, you are now exercising pride. There is always room for improvement. The goal should always be to improve as a student and never aim to be the guru, as the guru has reached the finale and has done it all. Pride is a derivative of ego. If you would like to learn more about the pitfalls of ego, I recommend you read the book "Ego is The Enemy" by Ryan Holiday. Humility is a beautiful trait and naturally gives off an aura that makes others want to be around you and work with you. Humility puts the ego to the back burner and helps you stay grounded in your core roots and principles. Despite your certain status or title, you are aware of those things but you don't allow them to define who you are. Once you lose the humility, you feel cocky or arrogant and feel like all of your blessings are because of you and your efforts. Sometimes in life things don't work out as planned, or life throws you unexpected triumphs. The humble person has no issue going down that same rope in which they came up because they treat people accordingly. If you are someone who is arrogant, once you fall or if you fall, others will laugh at you and no one will want to help you. Your arrogance will cause people to be happy that bad things happen to you. You'd also be a reminder to others that people shouldn't behave like you, otherwise there will be consequences.

Many will probably read this and blow it off saying, "the heck with those people." Well, not so fast. Remember, you cannot do this alone. All of us can practice humility by realizing that we don't personally control our own next breath, so let's not get things twisted and get a false sense of empowerment. There are people out there who work extremely hard yet things may not pan out in such ways as they do for us. That's nothing but a favor from the man upstairs. Humility allows you to be open-minded and engrave new innovations. Imagine working for a company but relocating to another state and finding another job. At this job they do the same tasks but their system or protocol is different from your previous employer. If you decide to approach the task closed-minded or feel you know everything due to the success at your previous job, then you can easily overlook tons of knowledge; therefore, causing you to possibly lose your job or cause unnecessary tension at your workplace. If you keep an open mind and take the humble route, you will realize that by trying their way and adapting to their protocol can lead to people trusting you and your opinions, eventually causing your colleagues to ask you for your suggestions and viewing you as a valuable asset to the company.

You can practice gratitude, and self-reflection can always keep you grounded. For some people, they prefer to learn things the hard way. Life experiences and failures teach them, but these experiences usually require you losing everything to regain a sense of humility.

Anything not growing is dead

Another aspect of mindset is realizing that growth is infinite. Whether you finished cum laude in school, or you were a dropout, both parties will have more room to grow and get better. The moment we feel we know everything; we start taking steps backwards. We have to always seek wisdom and be open-minded to new suggestions and ideas as well as always seeking to grow. Once you close your mind to new options, you stagger your own growth. We have both agreed that being closed-minded can be another form of getting in your own way and essentially blocking your blessings. This brings me back to one of my collegiate games at PVAMU. We defeated Alabama State University, a rival team who we had struggled to beat over the past few seasons. I had a stellar performance and made some huge plays for us defensively to seal the deal on the victory. My teammates and I were jumping around being full of energy and excitement as the clock winded down to conclude the game. Close by was my teammate Courtney Brown, aka "Buddha," strategically carrying the remainder of the ice-cold Gatorade cooler with me as we dumped it on the head of our head coach to share the love with him. The clock buzzed in conclusion and we shook hands with the opposing team and celebrated with one another. The game was our homecoming, so many of us went out to celebrate and reflect on the game with one another. We arrived back near campus, and were all surprised and in shock at what we would see. The game started around 4:00pm and concluded around 7:30pm. My teammates and I had gone out to have a good time and were returning home to finally get some rest. As we entered the campus, we had to drive by the coach's office to get to our onsite housing and we noticed the lights were on in his office and began looking at each other with a wild look of concern. My teammates and I thought something had to be wrong. The lights being on and coach's truck still parked outside, something was up and we had to go to check on coach (maybe he hurt himself and needed some help). As we tiptoed through the office, we found coach to be in the office 100% fine and listening to Lil Boosie's greatest hits on Pandora while reviewing our last game with a whiteboard full of potential game plans and adjustments for our upcoming opponent.

"Coach, are you alright? Don't you want to go home and get some sleep since we just won?" Courtney asked.

He didn't say anything, just a weird silence as a few of us looked at coach and then looked at each another searching for some sense of reaction. I decided to give it another try by breaking the silence and asked, "Coach, tonight's game was a good one, right? What did you think about the game tonight?" The words our coach shared with us have and will forever have a place in my heart. He paused the film stared at me for a few seconds. You could hear a pin drop in the room and I know my teammates were all looking to see where things would go next. Coach said, "you guys won, we did what we were supposed to do." We looked at each other, smiling and sharing handshakes in confirmation of coach's comment but he stopped us within seconds of celebrating to then say, "but now that one is behind us." I opened my mouth in an attempt to speak before coach cut me off. "But that doesn't count anymore, your biggest enemy is your previous success, we have to put that one behind us." And once again, we all looked around at one another in disarray to then hear coach conclude his thoughts. "Don't get comfortable." Coach turned his head back to the screen, pressed play on the film, and turned his music back up and asked that we return to our dorm rooms. I then learned the value of short-term memory—if you get stuck in your previous success or accomplishments, you can find yourself losing sight of the end goals. There is nothing wrong with a brief intermission of patting yourself on the back and celebrating the small wins, but you can never lose sight of the larger goal which for us was winning a championship.

NOTES

Chapter 4: Success leaves clues

The term success is similar to the word love, as most of us use it daily. The term can have so many different definitions. To some people, success is determined by the job/career status or if they have the corner office. To others, success is defined by having financial freedom. Some define success as loving your job and what you do every day despite the financial gains while others see success as being famous or having notoriety for what they do. Both terms, success and love, are all relative to the individual and there isn't a true right or wrong definition. As mentioned earlier there were hundreds of people interviewed and years of work put together to create this book and it has really amazed me how even within the same profession, many viewed successes on two completely different ends of the spectrum. Some say success was earning the respect of their peers. Others said it was retiring earlier than the expected age of 65, owning their home, being the superman of their family, earning passive income, and the list goes on and on. None of those are wrong, but my definition for success is identifying your gift/passion and utilizing it for the betterment of others. I believe that life itself is all about memories as we all have a certain time frame here on earth, and while our physical presence may leave, our memories and interactions with others will live forever.

We are in an era where everything is literally a few clicks away. There were times where if you didn't know anyone who did what you do, you would struggle to complete tasks or take a much longer time in getting things done. But now, we have knowledge and resources at our fingertips. We literally have people who earn millions of dollars working from home, creating online YouTube channels, and thousands of other ventures. In fact, there are people who are so intrigued by your gift and skill set, for example, playing video games or creating your product, that they will pay & donate money to watch you play or watch the behind the scenes version and experience in the life of you creating your product. You have an interest in makeup? No problem, visit your local bookstore, go on Youtube.com and spend countless hours indulging in your craft. These same principles apply to all crafts and professions. There was a time when these things were merely looked at as hobbies or extracurricular activities and wouldn't be considered a career or lucrative venture, so most people would find a job which they only tolerate while using their true passion as a weekend hobby. *Disclaimer*: I'm not saying this would be an overnight success nor am I saying everything will be an easy ride, but what I am saying is that if we want something bad enough, we should be willing to invest the time, energy, and money in ourselves.

Due to increased technology and ample resources, we have greater access to these things than of those in previous generations. For me, when I think of success, there are certain people that immediately come to mind. Floyd Mayweather, Michelle Obama, Tupac Shakur, Bernard Hopkins, LeBron James, and both of my grandmothers (Doris Peterson and Christine Reed). The names listed above vary not only in gender but also professions, ranging from elite athletes to executive directors to rappers/activists and the first lady of the United States. There are certain common denominators and factors they all possess that has led to their successes. Those denominators are what I refer to as clues. If you view Floyd Mayweather, currently a retired boxer and in a league of his own—earning a record of 50-0— you'd discover that boxing is far from a hobby. He is known for his random 2:00am-3:00am five mile runs on top of grueling workouts and is a master of his craft. Mayweather turned professional at age 19 with no college degree, just doing the best with what he knew and had. A ton of hard work combined with undebatable self-confidence and focus led him to now be considered by many as the greatest boxer of all time. In the previous chapter, we discussed a few of John Wooden's historic quotes. A lot of those can be found within the practice of Floyd Mayweather.

Now let's view Bernard Hopkins. He's from the streets of Philadelphia, had a rough upbringing, and made a few bad decisions that left him serving sometime in the penitentiary. While there, Hopkins began fighting and started making a name for himself as a renowned fighter. Once released, he continued his dominance in the ring and decided to change the way he would eat, train, and nourish his body, now adapting to the idea of viewing his body as his temple. He began meditation, improving his diet, valuing sleep, and being more conscious about the things he surrounded himself with spiritually, mentally, and physically because he realized that energy is contagious. He has a video which can be found on YouTube by searching "Bernard Hopkins' greatest advice ever" where he states, "I'm not that good. People think I'm that good, I'm not that good." He goes on to name several fighters who he says are better than him in regards to natural talents. He finishes the statement by saying, "but the difference is that I learned early on that if you keep your mind clean and don't get caught up in the bull crap that comes with success, you will be alright, and that's what I live by." Hopkins fought his last fight in 2014. Did I mention he was 49 years old at the time of the fight? He credits his accomplishments to practicing those topics he lives by.

Both of my grandmothers, Christine & Doris, grew up with a household full of siblings while being forced to grow up much faster than many at their age. They would later birth children of their own. They both had kids really young, carrying the burden of working numerous jobs to make ends meet while also aiming to be more than just a paycheck parent in a home full of children needing guidance, structure and attention. Through constant nights of prayers and headaches, they both went on to raise respectful children who are now honorable parents to their own kids. When the opportunity of giving up and throwing in the towel was presented, they allowed their kids and their faith in God to be their motivation to give it one more shot. These are two people who would constantly remind themselves of where they came from, never forgetting their victories and shortcomings. They would always push each other to be better. This mindset took them to greater heights than they could have ever imagined.

LeBron James. A household name from Akron, Ohio, he is a current NBA superstar and future hall of fame athlete. LeBron's resume remains in the upper echelon. That's not only on the court but also off it, utilizing his platform to create his personal brand, sparking the interest of many brands with regards to endorsements and even collaborating with Nike to create his own sneaker.

According to Sports Illustrated, 78% of former NFL players have gone bankrupt or are under financial stress because of joblessness or divorce within two years of retiring. Within five years of retirement, an estimated 60% of former NBA players are broke. James entered the NBA at 18 but was much wiser than many of his peers. He understood the grueling demand of the sport and how the league would find ways to get rid of you once your play starts declining or if your value was equal to or less than a younger player who they could trade for (usually for more cheaper money) or draft. He always reflects back to his rougher days from his childhood in order to stay grounded and uses that as fuel to give it one more shot, one more rep, one more whatever the applicable task may be. As opposed to getting caught up in the news articles and flashing lights, James quickly lived up to the hype and silenced the noise; if the exterior voices, fans/media, were his only source of motivation, he too could have gotten complacent as many have for decades before him. Lebron wanted to be "more than an athlete," so he used basketball as a platform and helped a few of his close friends attend college. They all wound up becoming business partners and created LRMR (Lebron, Randy, Michael, Rich), a business they all created together after James fired his previous agent which is now one of the top agencies and marketing companies in the world.

James has done movies, real estate, TV shows, and is a minority owner in professional soccer team, Liverpool. However, James also assisted in creating a school in his hometown in 2018 named the *I Promise School* (IPS). James credits his success to his wife (and high school sweetheart) and his close group of friends who were also his high school teammates. He utilizes his platform to help his friends make a name for themselves so they wouldn't have to live off his hype or fall off if he ever got traded or he when he makes the decision to retire. James was drafted in 2003 and is currently playing in his 16th season. Many athletes admire his ability to play at a high level for such a long period of time. Surprising to many, James spends nearly $1.5 million annually on taking care of his body from a mixture of trainers, chefs, recovery tools, and an array of other things he feels will give him a slight edge. The numbers seem insane but to play a sport which can earn you millions per year it only makes sense to take care of the breadwinner, your body.

Tupac Shakur, born as Lesane Parish Cooks, changed his name around a year after his birth. Tupac was born in East Harlem and died at the age of 25-years-old due to multiple gunshot wounds. Tupac is internationally recognized for his courage, leadership, and phenomenal music, all of which are still considered classics nearly 24 years after his death. Tupac stood firmly upon his beliefs and principles and had a way of reminding others that yes, one way may have worked to accomplish that goal, however, there are many ways to get things done; just because one person has accomplished it a certain way doesn't belittle nor make your way superior. It's simply just one way, out of many, to accomplish that specific task.

Tupac did get into his share of troubles as a teen, but he always considered himself a leader and believed in standing firmly on principalities. He also felt firmly that his purpose and passions were gifts to the world and were larger than him. Prior to his death, Tupac once cited, "I'm not saying I'm going to change the world, but I guarantee that I will spark the brain that will change the world." His image on my wall is a reminder that my voice is of purpose and I have enough power and impact to change someone else's life for the better. Irrespective of the number of social media followers we have, the car we drive, or anything of the sort, we all have a story and experiences that we can share to create an impact on someone else. Even something as small as a smile, a compliment or simply acknowledging someone's presence does more than we can imagine to some people.

Michelle Obama, raised in Chicago, Illinois, graduated cum laude at Princeton University. After graduating from Harvard Law school in 1988, she'd go on to meet Barack Obama, who'd later become the 44th President of the United States making her, of course, the First Lady. Amongst the list of phenomenal things, she has done I have always loved her vision and courage for women and seeking the opportunity given and utilizing her platform. Michelle knew that there was a short window of time that Barrack and her would be allowed to be present in the White House—despite him winning the second term. Michelle utilized that platform and promoted positivity and good in the world and became a role model for millions of people internationally.

Michelle had (and still has) a huge heart for the youth in creating the "let's move initiative," which helped fight obesity. She worked with schools to allow free breakfast for all students which has been proven to increase attention, test scores, attendance and even participation. She even helped 23 high schoolers create local gardens to grow their own organic fresh food in Washington, DC. As many, with their husband being the POTUS (President of the united states), she could have sat back and been content with fully supporting her husband as he led the country. Instead, though, she decided to use her undeniable voice to do things that she enjoyed, being selfless for the betterment of others, all while still being her husband's number one fan. She also used her platform to inspire women to view education as an asset. You don't need to have a Harvard degree, per say, but you should be educated and diligently work at whatever your heart desires. Michelle was also living proof that for women all things are possible and that they too have a voice in a world that's much more dominant for the masculine gender.

There are common denominators or "clues" for all of those mentioned in this chapter. They value their health and wellness, sacrifice short term gains and gratification for longevity, surround themselves with a good support system, stand firm on principles, are growth-minded and take pride in discipline. Although they may word it differently, many of these things are what I feel played a role in their success. I believe the devil is in the details, meaning it's the smaller things—the discipline and their mindset—that separates people who are *trying* to be successful from those who *are* successful. The small goals or habits these people created have led to 1% increases, but compounded day in and day out they lead to unimaginable blessings long term. The extensive career spans, endorsement deals, signing bonuses, million-dollar homes, movie appearances, ability to build schools, top selling albums or bestselling books are just the symptoms of years of self-confidence, belief in a higher power, relentless work ethic, anti-ego, discipline, a great supporting cast and the right mindset. (It sounds like a whole lot but it really isn't!) Another thing that stood out to me was, despite their financial gains and investments, they have all said or done things to promote time being their greatest investment. By taking the time to read through this book today, you are investing in yourself and already on the right track!

On the following page you will see an image created by my good friend Corey Pane (@coreypaneart on Instagram). We all have days where we

lack motivation or may need a reminder of what or why we're doing what we're doing. So, I keep this image hung up in my home as a daily reminder of why I started. The image also quotes "Stay Humble Eat Crumbs," which is a saying I created back in high school. It's an unwritten law for my friends and I that we are to remember to stay humble through it all and to not forget where we come from. Although many of my friends and I are from the inner cities of Fort Lauderdale, we aren't speaking about any hood or gang but more about not forgetting the core principles and upbringing that were instilled in us. We are where we are today because of good parenting; they all valued principles such as faith, respect, integrity, courage and wisdom. So those four words are what we recite to each other often when one of us may be having a hard time or if we feel that someone is starting to lose themselves. It's very common to receive a phone call or text message from one of us with the initials "S.H.E.C." If we receive that text, we all know it means to take a deep breath, reevaluate and get yourself back into focus and on track. You will also notice the fist which is a microphone, symbolizing the voice and how all of those people mentioned earlier used their voices or their platforms to shed light and inspire others. Inside the fist it states "success leaves clues." This has been the primary focus for this entire chapter.

You vs You

One of the first words an infant pronounces followed by ma-ma and da-da is NO. Surprisingly, though, as we get older, we seem to drift away from the no's and take them personally as if one no was the determining factor for our issues. Let's take a look at a number of people who were told no yet didn't allow one, two or 408 rejections stop them from what they believed in. Assuming you have used some sort of disinfectant spray such us Lysol, I'm sure you have heard of the company Formula 409. Contrary to popular belief, the name Formula 409 has nothing to do with an area code or pick three lottery selection. The name is nothing shy of two scientists who were resilient with their efforts and finally created the proper solution on their 409th attempt. They didn't allow negativity from their friends or supporting cast influence their decision to just give up and try something different. Rather, they kept their eyes on the prize. Steve Harvey quotes, "If you want to kill a big dream, tell it to a small-minded person." We have these amazing ideas in our head but we sometimes allow others to talk us out of our dreams, goals, and aspirations. More often than not, people are talking down on your goals due to their personal demons or insecurities. As kids, we are born with this massive imagination and our dreams and thoughts are beyond our wildest imagination and we attempt them with all our effort with little to no thought about what might happen.

Have you ever visited your ophthalmologists and optometrists? These two professions both play a role in providing vision and eye care for clients. They bring the client in for the initial consultation, go through a ton of tests & screenings and provide the client with vision assistance. This can be in the form of glasses, contacts, or vision therapy. If you ever have worn someone else's prescription glasses you have probably learned the hard way that everything is blurry, indefinite, foggy, and I have even seen instances where others were even hospitalized due to massive headaches from wearing someone else's glasses. You may have even been warned not to wear other people's glasses, because it can damage your eyes and possibly make you blind. That same concept applies to life. Not having clear vision in someone else's glasses doesn't make you blind. Those glasses were specifically made for them, so why try to see what they see. There's a reason why your dreams are your dreams. Just because it's yours and others don't see it doesn't mean your dreams (or your vision) is impossible. An infant never stops to complain about falling and never wanting to try to walk again. They simply dust off their shoulders, cry/shout—maybe even take a nap—and regain their confidence and give it another shot at a later time.

We live in a time where being average is the norm. You can party every weekend, only living in the now with no regards of your future, and do the bare minimum, but where will that get you as a professional? If you want to be good, rather, great, then you're going to have to go hard and battle through some storms to come out on top.

When was the last time you drove your car, sat on a plane, or even used your cell phone? Imagine if those creators didn't believe in themselves or if they allowed the insecurities of others to belittle them. The great Muhammad Ali spoke, saying "I am the greatest, I said that before I knew I was." Him believing in himself all along played a huge role in him going down in history as one of the best boxers to ever step foot in a ring. We are currently living in a generation where anything is possible. There are people less qualified than you who are making their dreams come true because they believe in themselves. Can you imagine how crazy it sounded when the Wright Brothers decided they wanted to fly a plane? Even still, imagine being one of the earlier passengers after its invention!? The Wright Brothers believed in themselves and wouldn't take no for an answer. Your mindset and your confidence set forth the standards in which you will live. If you become someone with low self-esteem then you will probably live life playing it safe in all things and allow fear to control your life, usually settling for something average or just less than you know you're worthy of.

The word FEAR can be looked at in two ways: <u>face everything and rise</u> or the less prominent answer of <u>fear everything and run</u>.

If you can't find the confidence to do it for yourself just think about the people who believe in you. You owe it to them to live up to your fullest potential. If anyone hasn't reminded you lately, we only have one go around on this thing called life. I know what you're thinking, "What if I don't make it or what if it doesn't happen?" or "I don't have the time" and countless other excuses that will no longer be accepted after reading this book. Let's shift our thinking for a second and answer these questions below:

What if it does happen?

What if it happens better than I imagined?

What if I was overthinking all along?

What if I spent my time & money more efficiently to reach my dream?

What if I meet a mentor along the way who guides me?

What if the man upstairs has given me all I needed and is waiting on me to do my part?

Another inhibitor of confidence/self-esteem is comparison. There's a quote that states "comparison is the thief of joy." *You cannot, you cannot, you cannot* compare yourself to others. This isn't a typo and is intentionally written three times to express the importance of not making this error that so many people make. You will never be enough or will always create an image for what's wrong when comparing yourself to others. In fact, you doing so is actually giving over the remote control of your happiness and peace to someone else. Therefore, you find yourself trading your joy for the false accusations of what you believe others are. Once again, we will refer to the social media comparison. Growing up, my mom had a rule that whatever happened in our house stayed in our house. This was self-explanatory and we weren't supposed to run out and tell our personal business to anyone who wasn't family or present when the situation occurred. This is the complete opposite of modern times, as every moment someone is pulling out their phone attempting to catch the next eye glazing moment—even something as small as a fist fight. When we were younger, we'd fight or argue and give one another a handshake or hug and the issue would be over right then and there. Now everything is recorded on phones and uploaded to various social media platforms in a matter of seconds. What's worse is that you no longer control the narrative and are now forced to relive this moment for as long as the desired audience finds it fit.

A huge negative about comparison is that we often compare our bloopers and imperfections to someone else's highlight. Have you seen someone post an eviction notice on social media? Or what about the credit score of 500 with the three to four accounts in collection? What about the failed acceptance letters from school's? Don't look for it because it won't happen. People (including myself) always share their highlights and greatest moments in life on their social media accounts. I view social media as another form where you can display your portfolio of work. We are all unique and special. According to World Population Review, there are over 7.5 billion humans on Earth yet there's only one person with our same fingerprint. That alone says a lot about our unique existence and purpose as individuals. There's only one reason why we're still alive, and it's because we've not yet completed our assignment on Earth. The only competitor should be the person in the mirror. You set your own pace, your own timeline and your own destination.

So, what if someone from your graduating class got a job in your field and maybe he/she was less qualified? It's okay, don't be jealous. Message them and congratulate them! Take the higher road and allow them to be an inspiration that your blessing is getting closer. You can be jealous of them and miss out on the next opportunity, the right opportunity, which can be a phone call hours later from another job who may offer you more money and better benefits. Don't be jealous or allow comparison to make you feel better or worse about your progress. You have to run your race because even though someone is winning in one category, they may be failing miserably in another.

We are all struggling in some aspect of life. I've had many talks with celebrities who we often put on these unreachable platforms. People who are often looked at as individuals who've "made it." What we generally see from those people is a lifestyle of flashiness, but if you are someone who they feel comfortable around and they bring you into their real world, a world of being recognized as a person and not a celebrity, you would realize that they are human like the rest of us. Some people spend their entire lives wanting to be them, to have the financial freedom and notoriety they have in their field. As crazy as it sounds, however, many of them want to be you. They want to be away from the limelight, they want genuine relationships, genuine love, privacy and the ability to trust. Many celebrities will tell you that their status comes with a lot, from everybody randomly recording you when they see you to undiscussed expectations and even dealing with loneliness and depression. There's always someone approaching you with their problem, genius million-dollar plan or guilt trip, and now you feel responsible for fixing it all. These are a few reasons why many who win the lottery gain a drug problem or commit suicide. You have people who have the money and everything the world says they need to be successful yet are extremely insecure and lack confidence in themselves. You have women who may make a few hundred bucks a month but her faith and emotional durability is as strong as an ox.

This next one I see the most (due to my profession) are people who've worked so hard to make tons of money annually and have great investment portfolios but are dealing with health risks that have accumulated over the years. They did not take care of themselves and are now on all sorts of breathing machines, pills or assisted devices fighting for their lives. This doesn't include the time and money that's now invested in seeing doctors and other specialized professionals. We are humans and we all struggle with things in our lives.

I personally struggle with trust and forgiveness. I don't trust many people which causes me to never let people get too close to me. This doesn't exclude family members, I can't name many people who I do trust, and if you are one of the few to get through the cracks and you do something thing that seems untrustworthy, I don't do well with forgiving you even if it's years later. I'm one of those people who forgives but never forgets. The way someone made me feel after being nothing but good to them is something that will always sit in the back of my head. We'll be cool, and I will speak to and be respectful toward you, but that hesitation to let you in will always wonder around my consciousness.

Don't forget your blinders

Have you ever been to a casino or any race track where you see horses racing at laser speeds while the equestrian rapidly conducts the horse to the finish line? The history of horse racing can go as far back as the early 1500-1600s. There are about four different types of racehorses ranging from Thoroughbred, Friesian, Appaloosa, and Quarter Horse. Originally, racing didn't take place in the US until around the late 1800s. By the late 1890s, there was a little over 300 tracks in the US. As with many things, once there is a small window or market for something it explodes. Sports betting and gambling were no different. People would travel worldwide to bet unbelievable amounts of money on horses. This became a huge money stream for the horses and the venue as the gamblers were required to pay a house fee. This also brought out the inner competitor in many people causing them to invest money seeking mentors, in the horse's physical training, organic diets and the latest data. This doesn't include the fees of actually purchasing a horse of good quality which can markedly increase in cost and rates for finding the best equestrians to guide the horses. As with humans, the horses have additional day to day needs such as shelter, bathing, vaccination, etc. There were people who would risk hundreds of millions of dollars on races that would last 12-17 seconds (assuming this was a $1/8^{th}$ of a mile race) depending on the horse's speed. On paper, this theory makes a ton of sense: you only get out what you put in so if you want the best horse you have to sell your home, empty your retirement plan and go all in on race horse #1. That was a common mistake many people made and the turn out would be tough for the eyes to watch. Gamblers would invest their money and on the day of the race some horses wouldn't leave the stall. Some would get to the finish line and turn around while others would be gunning for first place, see poop on the ground or see another horse who fell and just stop and focus on the poop or the fallen horse, practically eliminating any hopes of winning. It wasn't until one day horse blinders were created so now the only thing within the horse's sight was the finish line. Blinders restricted their peripheral vision and eliminated distractions. The horse's only focus was keeping his eye on the prize and finishing the race. Again, each horse did have genetic limitations due to its breed, but the only way each horse can run to its maximal potential was by eliminating distractions and keeping the finish line in its focus.

This same concept can be applied to our lives as humans. We should always invest in ourselves. You should be putting yourself in the best position to win, allowing a chance for a large return on investment. There will always be distractions, it's inevitable. Someone will always be lurking with their hands out wanting something from you, wanting to slow you down on your path to greatness, but if we put our blinders on—despite genetic limitations we may have, like the horse—we can focus on maximizing our potential and becoming the most dynamic versions of ourselves, realizing that we are our only competitors and the battle is—and always will be—between you and you.

NOTES

Chapter 5: Who you are vs what you do

Well, you've made it to the final chapter and I hope you have opened your mind and gained a different perspective compared to before you opened the book. Ask yourself the following questions:

Who am I?
What are my core values?
Why do I do what I do?
Who do I do it for?

Now ask yourself these questions:

What's your current occupation?
What do you do for fun?

These questions were strategically put together, as the first few questions are based on your character and who you are while the second set of questions pertain to what you do. We all share the same common 24 hours in a day and research has suggested that we should spend roughly seven to nine of them sleeping per night. This leaves us with around 15-17 hours and usually eight of those hours are spent at work. We are now left with around seven to eight hours, but once you include the time we usually spend on lunch breaks, commuting to and from work, never ending deadlines, policy renewals, budget cuts, or maybe it's peak season for your company, it can't be facile to mix the two as one entity. Not to mention, if you're a parent you have to deal with events in the community that have their own set of time-consuming obligations.

We all love incentives and a sense of accomplishment so we work relentlessly for the next raise, the corner office, a parking spot, the special badge of honor amongst your peers, etc. While all these things have their place, everything can be the enemy if consumed outside of moderation. As a fitness professional, I constantly speak to clients about the importance of hydration but even something as simple as water can be deadly in the wrong hands or in excess amounts. Kids drown from swimming, tornadoes and hurricanes— all things water related; while a lot rarer than the aforementioned, there are scenarios where you can have diminishing returns or even death from too much water. The devil is always in the dosage. The same water that grows the farmers crops is the same water in excess that floods the grounds and wastes millions of dollars in produce. This same philosophy applies to us daily, we just may overlook it.

There aren't many things I regret in life because everything that seemed disastrous at one time, in hindsight, helped make me unapologetically the person I am and, most importantly, the person I am becoming. I would like to think the same applies to you. I was hugely disappointed in myself for the way I responded once the air was removed from the ball and I was no longer a student athlete. I honestly felt like my life was over and had no sense of direction. I associated all of my self-worth and value to playing football and chasing down ball carriers as if that was all I was called on to do. I know now how silly and naive that was of me to even imagine that something so minute in the grand scheme of things would be all that I was capable of. Playing sports and being a student athlete was simply a platform and not solely who I was as a person. From a young age, my mother and grandparents instilled in me not to judge a book by its cover and to not be jealous and not look down on someone due to their current status, financial gains, or anything related. Consequently, those same principles are not applied to everyone so there are many people who will only speak to you due to your current job or position or maybe due to a current affiliation you have with someone or something. However, once those things change, they will be on to the next thing smoking or the next person they feel has it going on. My peers and I, we like to call those people "groupies." This term has been commonly used to refer to women but, contrary to popular belief, there has been a huge epidemic of males who possess such qualities.

Moments as such take me back to my tenure at PVAMU. Our biggest rival was the Texas Southern Tigers. We played them annually on the first game of the season which was coined the Labor Day Classic. There were years when we beat Texas Southern and we could do no wrong. The cafeterias would be kept open for us longer, we would have pep rallies; the football players were the golden children for those brief days. Though, if we went out the following week and lost a game or perhaps kept the game too close to an opponent that we should have beaten easily, then you may have chosen to eat at home that week or purchase some headphones from the bookstore before you went into class or the cafeteria because you were going to get attacked by the sideline head coaches of the century: the student body and staff. Many of these sideline head coaches had never played a snap or couldn't tell you the difference between a wide receiver screen and a play action, but were so quick to judge you on your performance, what play should be called, how much the team sucks, who is out of position and whatever else they felt applicable at that moment in time.

The late John Wooden (who is one of the winningest coaches in history, known for his insane mindset, details, and approach towards the game) would often give his team many talks that later turned into quotes. One of those quotes was "Talent is God given. Be humble. Fame is man-given. Be grateful. Conceit is self-given. Be careful."

Those very same people who were once our biggest fans were now walking by without speaking, acting the complete opposite from their performance from previous weeks. This transitions me to the next quote of Coach Wooden's: "You can't let praise or criticism get to you. It's a weakness to get caught up in either one." This quote is intertwined with the principle that my mother instilled in me as discussed in the intro about always seeking a happy medium, never too high never too low, because if you aren't careful you could hand over your happiness to others and that will always be a rollercoaster—they will treat you based upon how beneficial you are to them. If they can't use you or get something from you then they'll treat you accordingly, but if they feel you provide something of value they will treat you different, take you out to eat, invite you to happy hour, host pep rallies, and even add your name to the guest list for the party.

My mother engraved those in me but I had mistakenly combined my core values and character with my current situation. You can be a lawyer, doctor, cashier, coach, professional athlete, or CEO today, and decide to go switch professions tomorrow—does that no longer make you educated, wise, resilient, a parent, a role model, a believer, or a hard worker amongst other traits? Yes, I see you, it's okay to smile, because we both know the answer to that. Those chills that you felt while rereading that last sentence was the sign of confirmation that you've been looking for. I challenge you to review the questions answered at the beginning of this chapter and implement your core values into your daily lives.

Be more concerned with your character than your reputation, because your character is what you really are, while your reputation is merely what others think you are." - John Wooden.

I'd like to thank you for taking the time to pick up this book. I pray that this book inspires you to take time out to reflect and understand the distinction between the two.

NOTES

Jerome Howard was born in Fort Lauderdale, Florida and is an alumnus of Prairie View A&M University where he obtained a Bachelor of Science degree in human performance. Howard received a full athletic scholarship and would finish his tenure as an All-American linebacker and multiple record holder. He is now CEO of Dynamic Performance Development, a fitness company specializing in meeting the client at their current level of fitness and developing their performance in order to create the most dynamic version of themselves. Howard writes about his experiences and those of others from numerous professions about several times where they've been stuck asking, "SO NOW WHAT"? Jerome shares deep insight on success and general fulfillment in life.

Contact
Email info.dynamicpd@gmail.com
www.traindynamicpd.com
Social media
Instagram @Dynamic_pd
Facebook @Dynamicpd
Twitter @Dynamic_DPD

Made in the
USA
Middletown, DE